8 Days in a Coma:
"A Journey Between Heaven and Hell"

By Jeremy Cooper

8 Days in a comA:
A Journey
Between
Heaven and HeLL

By
Jeremy Justin Cooper

To Jennifer, My North Star in stormy seas, who said "I do" on that blessed April day in 2016. You've stood by me through calm waters and raging storms, Through health and heart attacks, Through every adventure and every challenge. Your love guides me home like a lighthouse in the dark. To William, Diamond My greatest treasures, more precious than any find in all my years of treasure hunting. You make your old pirate dad proud every single day. Together with your mom, you all give meaning to every voyage I take. You are my reason for fighting back from those eight days, my motivation for sharing this story, and my assurance that heaven awaits us all. God blessed this pirate with the finest crew any captain could ask for. With eternal love,

Your Captain

Chapter List

Prologue:
A
Pirate's Testament

Chapter 1
The Valtine's Day Massacre
February 14th, 2023:
When Time
Stood Still

Chapter 2:
The Ward Between Worlds
Journey to the 1930s Hospital
The Nurse and the Investment Advice

Chapter 3:
Locked in the '80s
Detroit Jail and Timeless TV
Bargaining for Freedom

Chapter 4:
Trapped in the Narrow Place
The Trailer Home Prison
Evil Wearing a Caretaker's Mask

Chapter 5:

Time's Twisted Mirror

The Chicago Hotel
A Wedding Out of Time

Chapter 6:

Screens in the Sky

The Future Hospital
The Quest for Milk

Chapter 7:

The Devil's Power Outage

Breaking Free

The Catholic Hospital Steps

Full Circle with the Nurse

Chapter 8:

Treasures Between Heaven and Hell

Lessons from Beyond

A Pirate's Path to Faith

Epilogue:

A Pirate's Guide to Heaven
and Hell
(And All Ports Between)
Still Waiting for That Ober Eats Delivery!

Thank you

Have a good read

8 DAYS IN A COMA

Chapter 1

A Valentine's Day Massacre

February 14th, 2022, dawned like any other Illinois winter day in Peoria. The morning light struggled through gray clouds, casting weak shadows across my bedroom as I fought against the growing certainty that something was terribly wrong. As someone who'd danced with diabetic comas before, I knew the warning signs – but this felt different. My white blood cells were waging war inside my body, and I was losing.

JEREMY JUSTIN COOPER

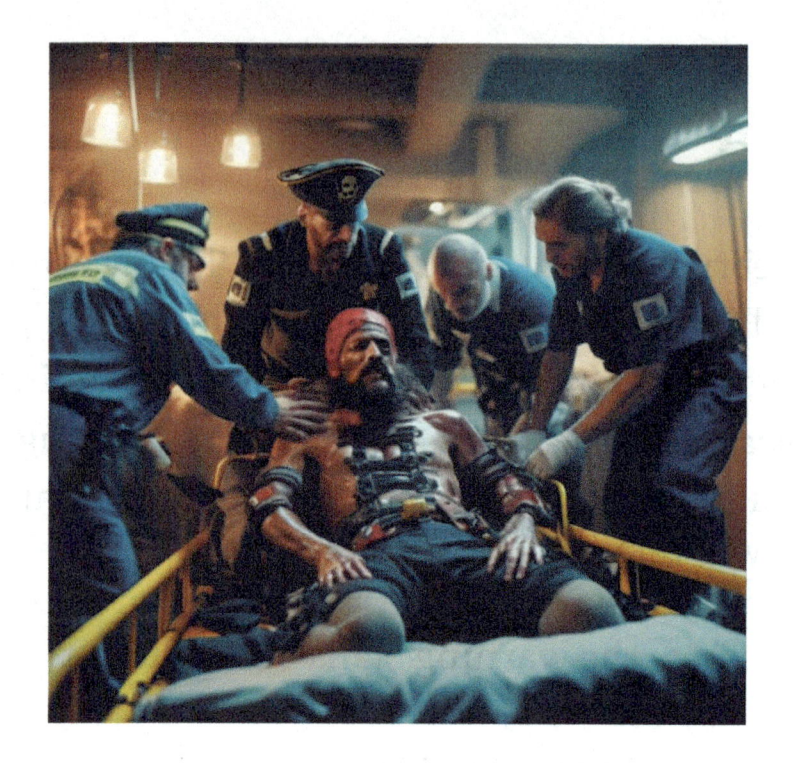

The day that should have been filled with love and celebration with Jennifer, my wife of nearly seven years, instead became a descent into a realm between life and death. We'd been through health scares before – diabetes had taught us resilience – but the look in Jennifer's eyes told me this time was different.

JEREMY JUSTIN COOPER

My strength ebbed away like a tide pulling back from shore. Simple tasks became monumental challenges. Even reaching for my phone to call for help felt like lifting a mountain. The sound of my voice asking for emergency services seemed to come from somewhere far away, as if I was already beginning to drift from this world.

The paramedics arrived quickly, their heavy boots thundering up our stairs, equipment rattling with each step. They were professionals, I could see it in their movements, but my size presented a challenge. At 42 years old, I wasn't a small man, and navigating my frame down the narrow staircase would require precision.

JEREMY JUSTIN COOPER

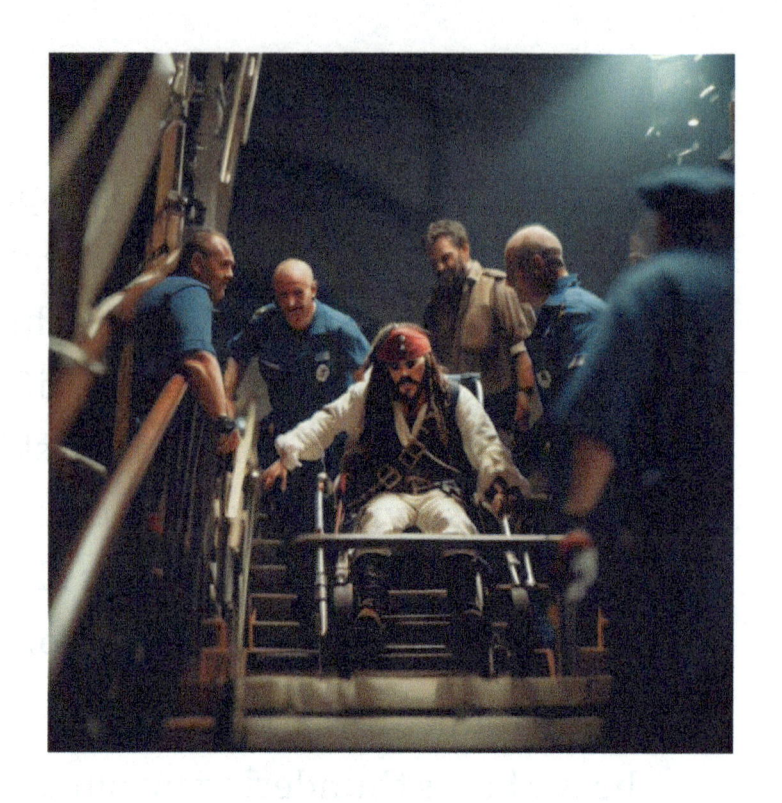

That's when it happened. Halfway down, I felt the gurney shift. But enough to send a jolt of panic through my system. That moment of terror, that split second of feeling unsecured, triggered something catastrophic inside my chest. My heart, already stressed from the infection raging through my body, couldn't handle the surge of adrenaline The last sensations I remember were vivid yet fragmentary: the bitter bite of February air as they wheeled me outside, the sound of Jennifer's voice somewhere behind me, the metallic clang of the ambulance doors.

JEREMY JUSTIN COOPER

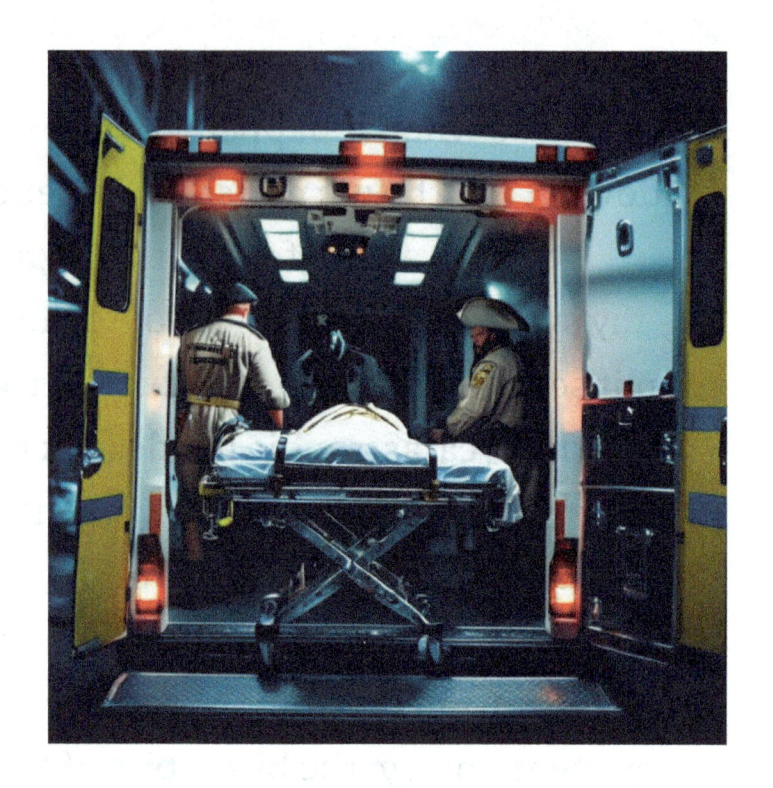

Then darkness swept in, pulling me into what would become an eight-day journey through realms no living person was meant to see. When consciousness finally returned eight days later, my first words to Jennifer weren't about pain or confusion.

Instead, I looked into her tear-filled eyes and asked, "Are you dead too?" It wasn't delirium speaking – after what I'd experienced, it was a perfectly rational question.

For eight days, I had traversed the space between heaven and hell, experiencing visions and encounters that would forever change my understanding of life, death, and faith. I had seen evil wearing many faces, felt the restraints that bound me in multiple timelines, and witnessed both the darkest and most divine aspects of existence.

JEREMY JUSTIN COOPER

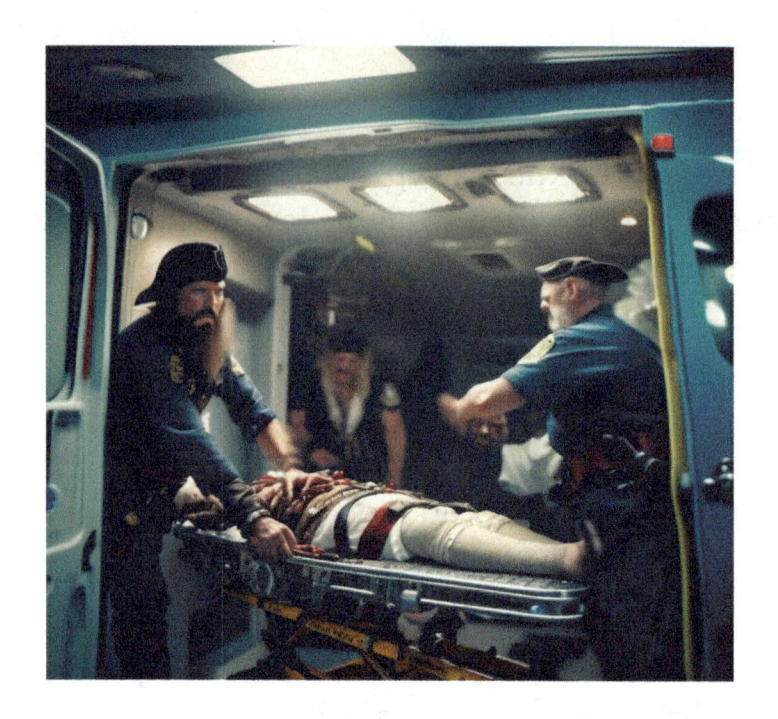

When consciousness finally returned eight days later, my first words to Jennifer weren't about pain or confusion. Instead, I looked into her tear-filled eyes and asked, "Are you dead too?" It wasn't delirium speaking – after what I'd experienced, it was a perfectly rational question. For eight days, I had traversed the space between Heaven and Hell, experiencing visions and encounters that would forever change my understanding of life, death, and faith. I had seen evil wearing many faces, felt the restraints that bound me in multiple timelines, and witnessed both the darkest and most divine aspects of existence.

JEREMY JUSTIN COOPER

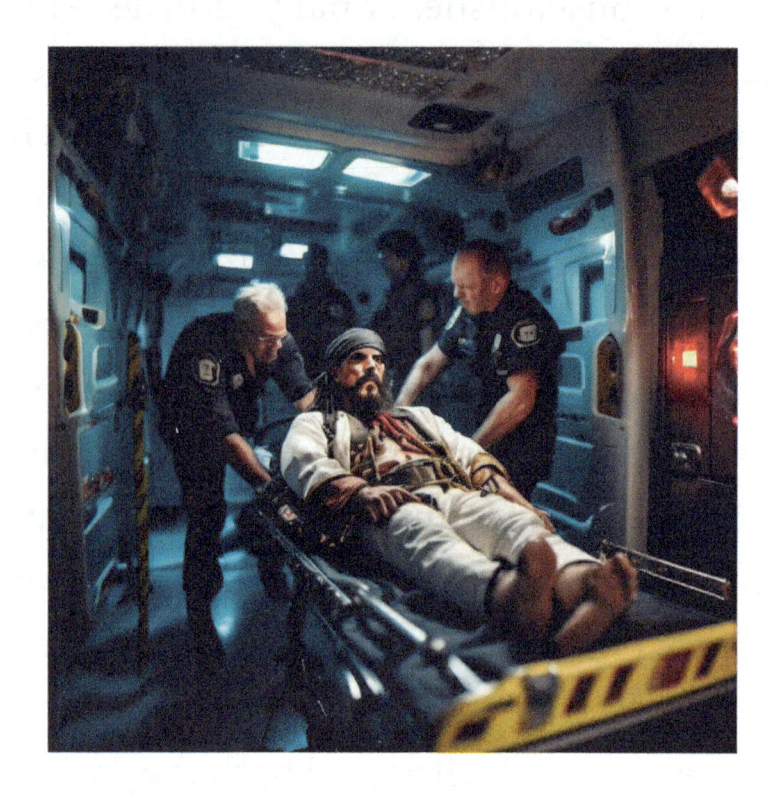

This is my story – a testament to the reality of both heaven and hell, and the precarious space that lies between them. A journey that began with a medical emergency but became something far more profound: a spiritual awakening that would shake the very foundations of my belief system. What I experienced in those eight days would change me forever. And if you're willing to join me on this journey, it might change you too. Because what I learned in that space between worlds is that God is real, heaven is real, and hell is real – and none of us should wait until we're caught between them to make our choice.

JEREMY JUSTIN COOPER

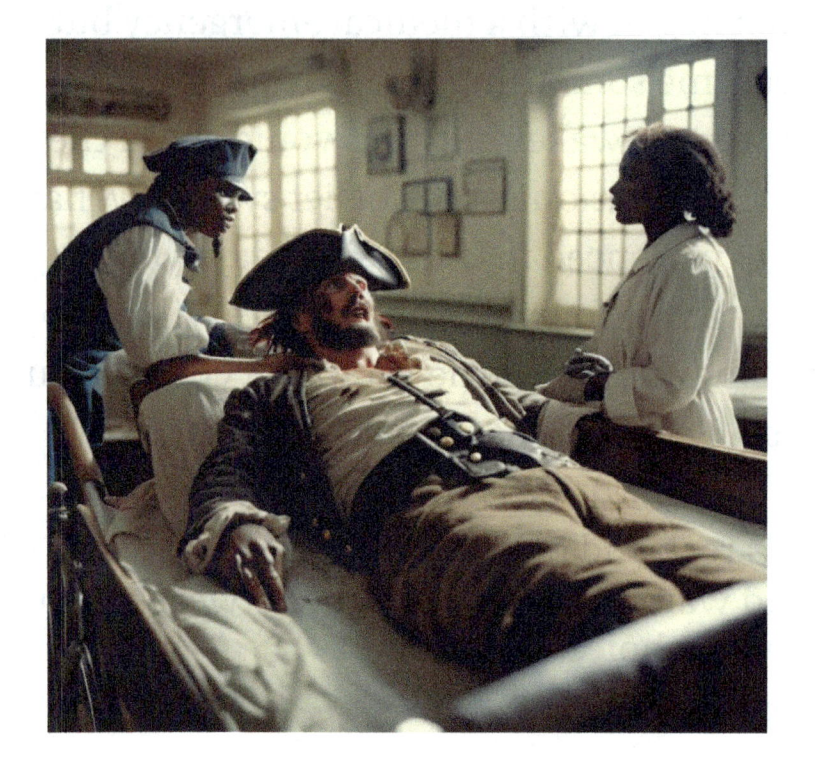

CHAPTER 2:

The Ward

Between

Worlds

JEREMY JUSTIN COOPER

Time doesn't flow normally between heaven and hell. One moment I was in the bitter February air of 2022 Peoria, and the next, I found myself thrust backwards through time into what appeared to be the 1930s or '40s. The transition was jarring - like being thrown from a speeding train into a black-and-white photograph suddenly come to life.

The hospital ward materialized around me with haunting clarity - a long room stretching perhaps sixty feet, with harsh fluorescent lights casting sickly shadows across institutional green walls. Two rows of gurneys lined the space, each one occupied, each patient firmly secured with restraints that seemed more appropriate for a prison than a place of healing. The room was perhaps thirty feet wide, but it felt narrower, as if the very walls were pressing in on us.

JEREMY JUSTIN COOPER

The air hung heavy with the sounds of old - time music - the kind my grandparents would play on their vintage record player, scratchy melodies that spoke of simpler times. G M orchestra, maybe, or something even older, the music floating through the stale air like ghosts of happier days. It was the kind of music that should have been
comforting, but in this setting, it only added to the surreal atmosphere.

JEREMY JUSTIN COOPER

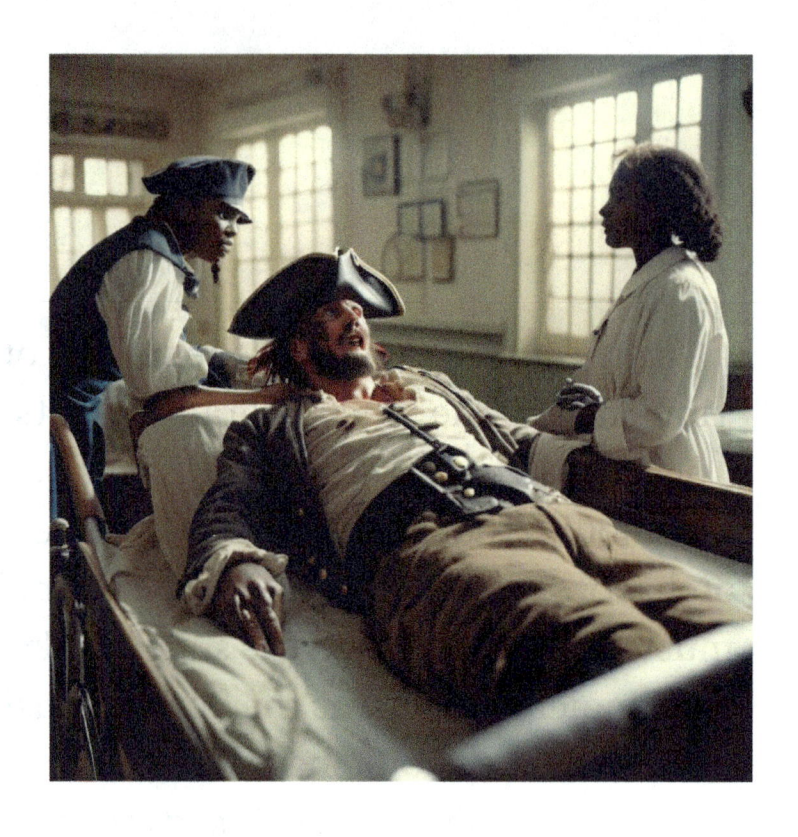

Black nurses in crisp, period-appropriate uniforms moved between the beds with practiced efficiency. Their shoe slicked against the linoleum floors in a steady rhythm that seemed to counterpoint the old-time
music. They were professional, focused, but there was something else in their manner a knowledge of things beyond my understanding.

JEREMY JUSTIN COOPER

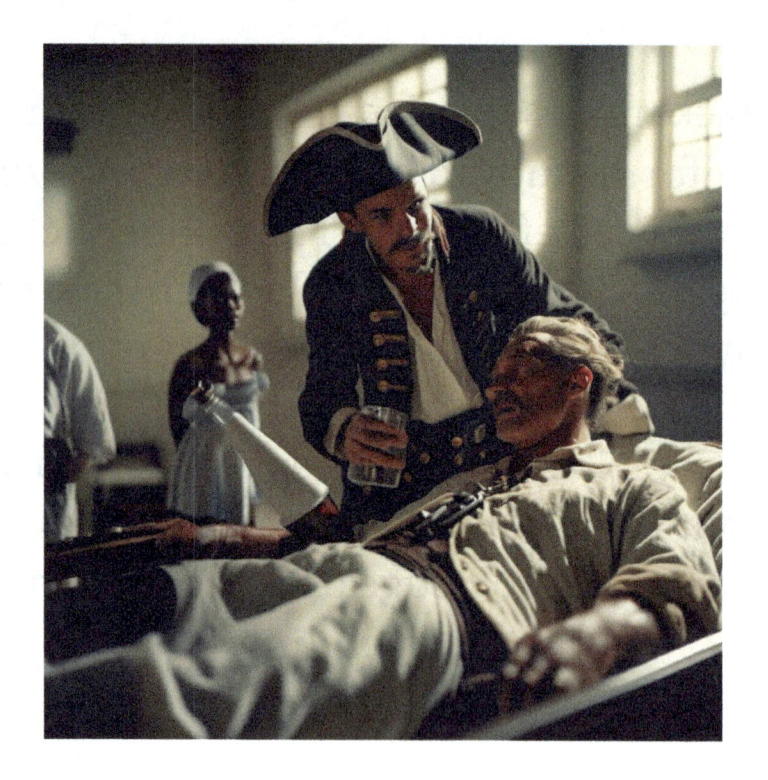

My throat burned with an unquenchable thirst that seemed to consume my entire being. "Can I have some milk?" The words became my mantra, repeated endlessly into the sterile air. "Please, just some milk!" Such a simple request, yet it felt like I was asking for salvation itself. While other patients lay silent in their restraints - were they even real patients? I continued my desperate pleas, feeling increasingly isolated in my awareness of this strange reality.

JEREMY JUSTIN COOPER

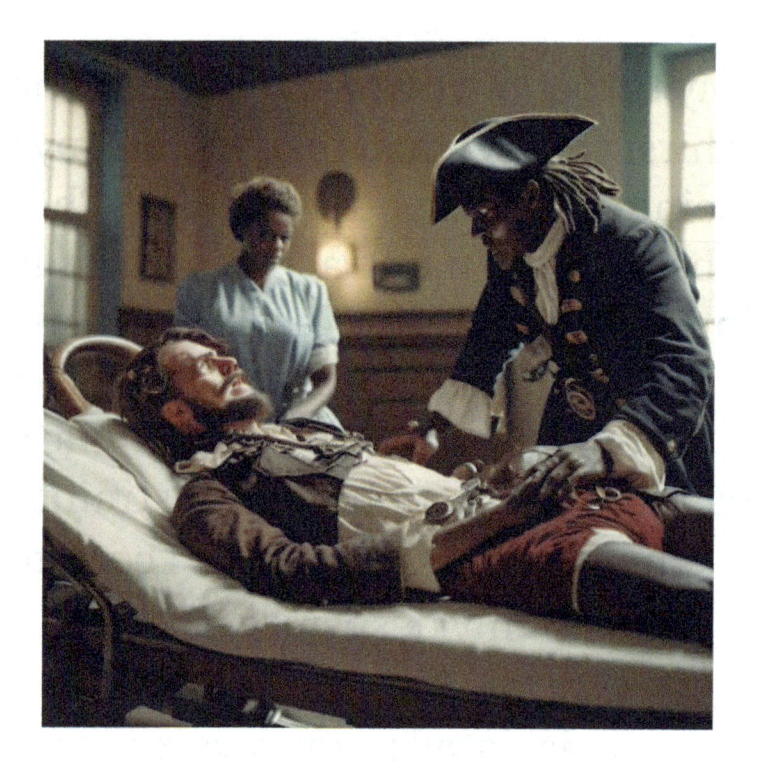

Then something changed. One nurse - a kind-faced Black lady with eyes that seemed to hold ancient wisdom - heard me. She approached my bedside, and for the first time since this nightmare began, I felt a connection to another soul in this strange realm. "Am I doing, okay?" she asked, showing the first real concern, I'd encountered.

The words poured out of me like a flood breaking through a dam: "I don't think I belong here. Where's my wife? Where is Jennifer? Where's William? Where's Diamond? Who are you, and where am I?" My family had become my anchor to reality, and their absence felt like a physical pain, a hollow space in my chest where my heart should be.

JEREMY JUSTIN COOPER

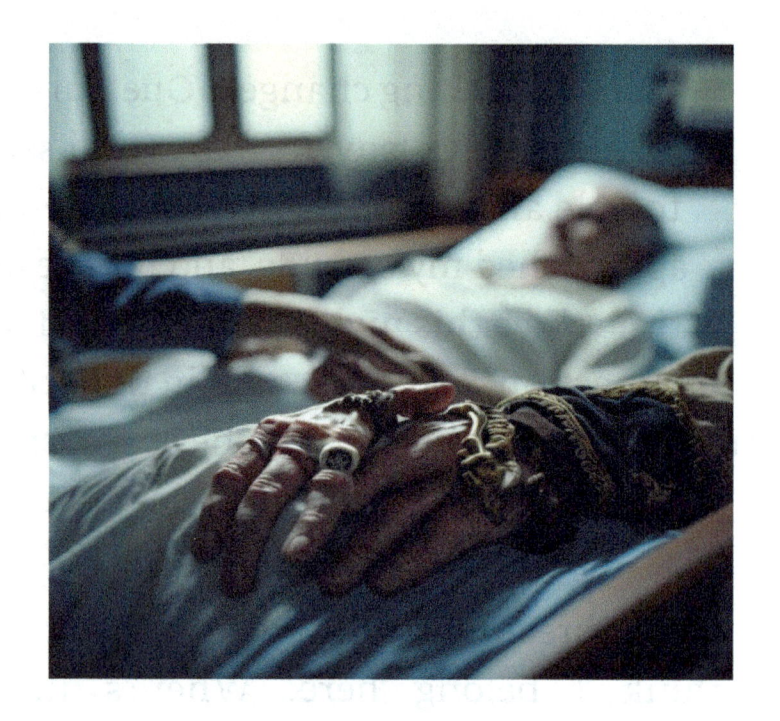

Her response was both gentle and cryptic: "You're here because you need to be here." Those words sent me into a panic, thrashing against the restraints that held me to the gurney. In my desperation, I tried to bargain with her, offering knowledge of the future like a modern-day Cassandra. $20,000 directly in stocks. Your family will be millionaires. When Amazon comes along, invest there too. Help these startups, and your family will never want for anything."

She seemed to consider my words, her eyes showing a glimmer of understanding that went beyond the normal nurse-patient relationship. She made several attempts to help, her hands hovering over my restraints, but something always held her back. Later, I would learn that my struggles in this vision corresponded to my physical attempts to dislodge the life-saving equipment during my heart surgery in the real world. The restraints weren't just part of the vision - they were keeping me alive.

JEREMY JUSTIN COOPER

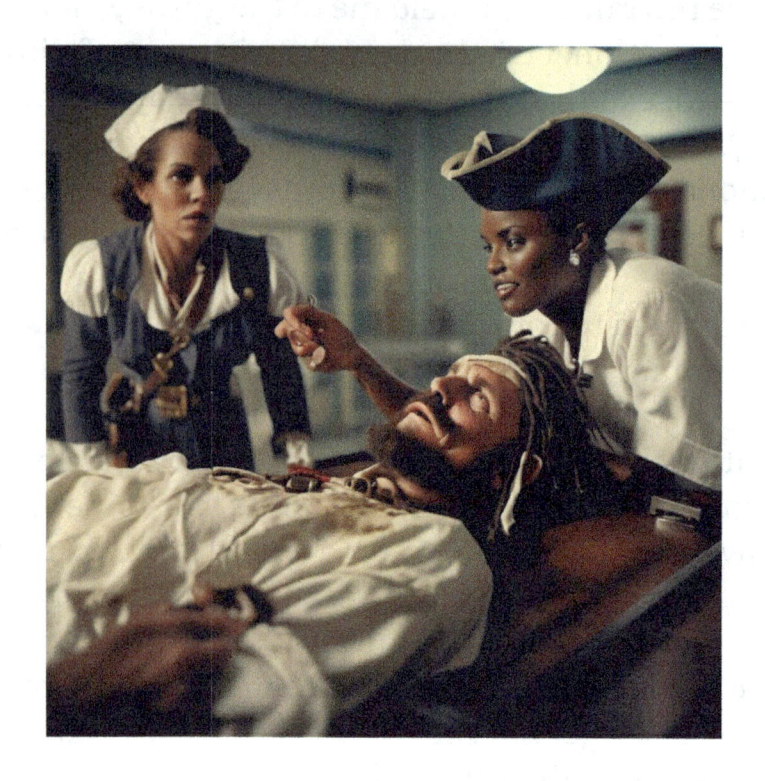

"Please," I begged, my voice cracking with emotion, "I need my wife. I miss her. I love her. I want her so bad." The raw emotion in my voice seemed to echo off the walls, creating a chorus of desperation. Jennifer wasn't just my wife – she was my lifeline to reality, my proof that somewhere beyond this nightmare, real life still existed.

JEREMY JUSTIN COOPER

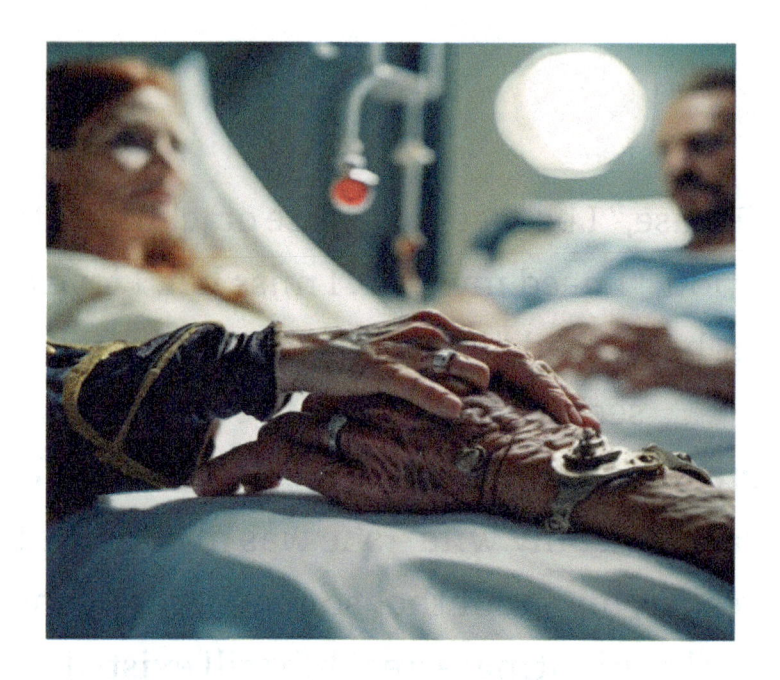

But just as the nurse reached toward me, her face showing A mixture of compasion and something deeper – was it recognition? – everything went dark. The ward, the music, the other patients, all of it dissolved into a darkness that seemed to pull me toward whatever reality awaited me next In that moment of transition, I didn't know if I was truly experiencing the past, if I was dead, or if I was caught in some terrible in-between place. All I knew was that this was just the beginning of my descent into a reality where time had no meaning, and the boundaries between Heaven and Hell grew increasingly blurred.

JEREMY JUSTIN COOPER

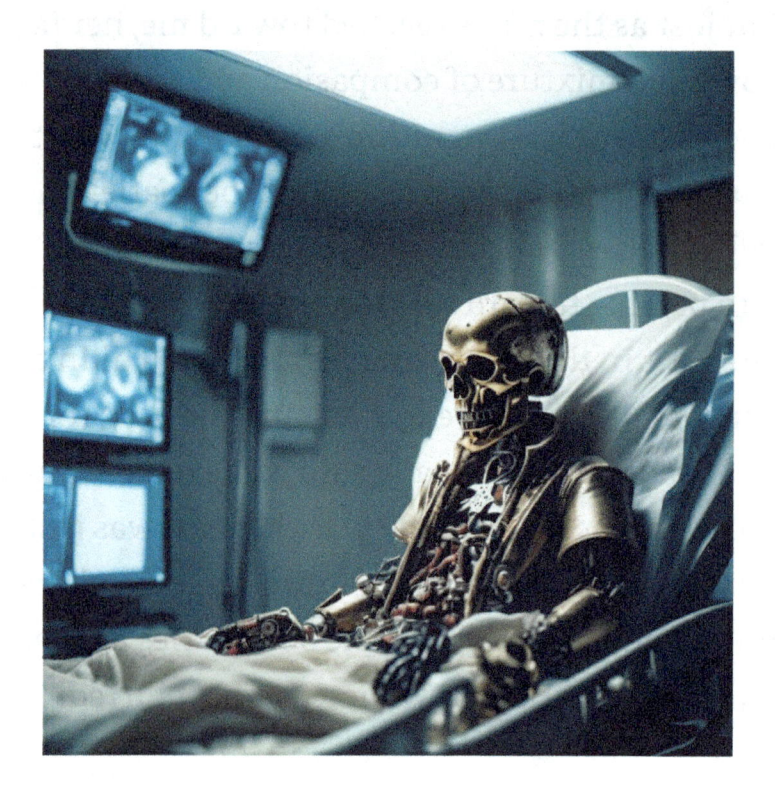

What I didn't realize then was that each of these visions, these seemingly random jumps through time and space, was teaching me something profound about the nature of existence itself. And my journey through the veil was only beginning.

JEREMY JUSTIN COOPER

CHAPTER 3:

LOCKED UP IN THE '80S

JEREMY JUSTIN COOPER

The darkness that swallowed the 1930s hospital ward gave way to the harsh glare of fluorescent lights and the unmistakable smell of institutional disinfectant that unique mixture of bleach, sweat, and despair that only a jail can produce. The processing cell of a 1980s Detroit jail materialized around me, a place I'd never been in my waking life, yet here I was, experiencing every gritty detail as if I'd been sentenced to relive someone else's memories. The cell was a constant buzz of activity, like a beehive built of concrete and steel. New inmates cycled through processing in an endless parade of misery and defiance. In the background, a mounted TV played a bizarre marathon of daytime television

JEREMY JUSTIN COOPER

Oprah offering life advice while Sally Jessy Raphael's distinctive red glasses peered out at an audience that existed decades ago. The programs created a surreal soundtrack to my imprisonment, a reminder that this was the 1980s, a time when I should have been a child, not a grown man fighting for his soul in a, "Detroit holding cell."

JEREMY JUSTIN COOPER

Unlike my previous vision where physical restraints bound me to a hospital gurney, here I was confined by something more substantial – concrete walls and steel bars that seemed to pulse with their own malevolent energy. The cell was both crowded and impossibly lonely, filled with souls who either couldn't or wouldn't acknowledge my existence. So, this was as both crowded and impossibly lonely, filled with soul who either couldn't or wouldn't acknowledge my existence. "I'll trick on anybody you want," I found myself bargaining with the detectives, my voice taking on the desperate edge of a man who knows he's trapped in the wrong reality. "I'll infiltrate whoever you need. Just let me out – I must find my wife!" Jennifer remained my North Star, the one constant I sought through every shifting timeline. But these detectives, faces I'd never seen in my waking life yet now seemed burned into my memory, were both impossibly obviously wrong – like actors playing their parts in a cosmic drama designed just for me.

JEREMY JUSTIN COOPER

8 DAYS IN A COMA

The processing cell became a twisted
theater of souls, with an endless parade of new
arrests coming through. Some faces showed the
same confusion I felt, lost souls trapped in this
limbo between times. Others, though – they
were different. They seemed to relish the chaos,
finding joy in tormenting those who couldn't
escape. It was my first clear glimpse of how good
and evil could exist side by side in this between-
place, neither fully heaven
nor completely hell, but something more
terrifying – a place where both tried to
claim dominion over lost souls

8 DAYS IN A COMA

JEREMY JUSTIN COOPER

Time stretched and warped like a fun house mirror. Hours felt like days, yet somehow, I remained trapped in that same processing cell, watching the same TV shows loop endlessly, hearing the same conversations repeat like a broken record. I was a man from 2022, a small business owner who sold pirate-themed treasures online, now trapped in a 1980s purgatory where no one from my time could possibly find me.

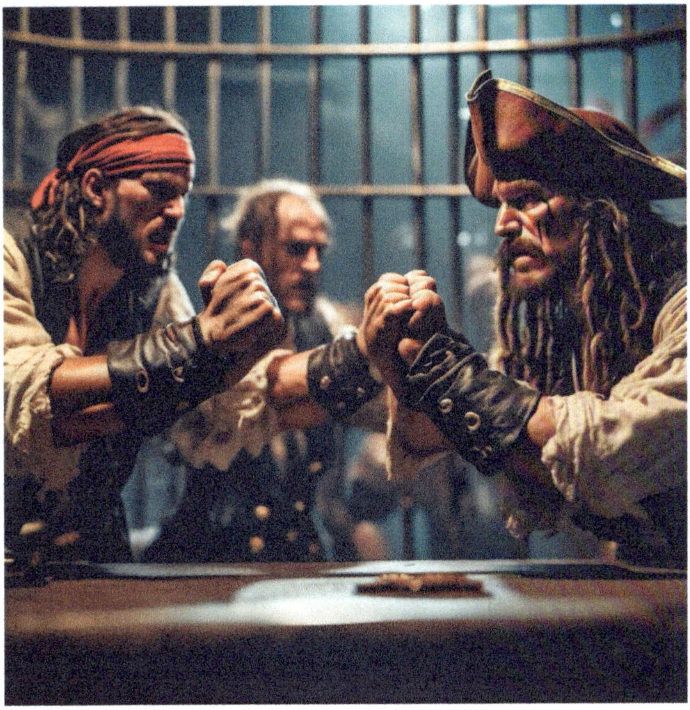

The fight, when it came, erupted with the sudden violence of a summer storm. I don't remember how it started or who threw the first punch. The details blur like rain on a windshield, but I remember the impact, the taste of copper in my mouth, and the darkness rushing in like a tide. As consciousness faded, I felt myself being pulled toward yet another reality, another scene in this cosmic play of redemption and damnation.In that moment, suspended between darkness and light, between one hellish reality and the next, I realized something profound: these weren't just random visions or drug-induced hallucinations from my hospital bed. Each scene was teaching me something about the nature of good and evil, about the thin line between heaven and hell, about the choices we make and the consequences that follow.

8 DAYS IN A COMA

Chapter 4

Trapped
In A
Narrow
Place

8 DAYS IN A COMA

As the jail cell faded into darkness, I understood that my journey was far from over. Like a pirate navigating treacherous waters, I was being forced to chart a course through realities I never knew existed, each one testing my faith, my love for Jennifer, and my very understanding of what it means to be alive - or dead - or somewhere in between.

The darkness claimed me once again, but this time, I knew another vision awaited. What I didn't know was whether the next reality would bring me closer to heaven or drag me further into hell.

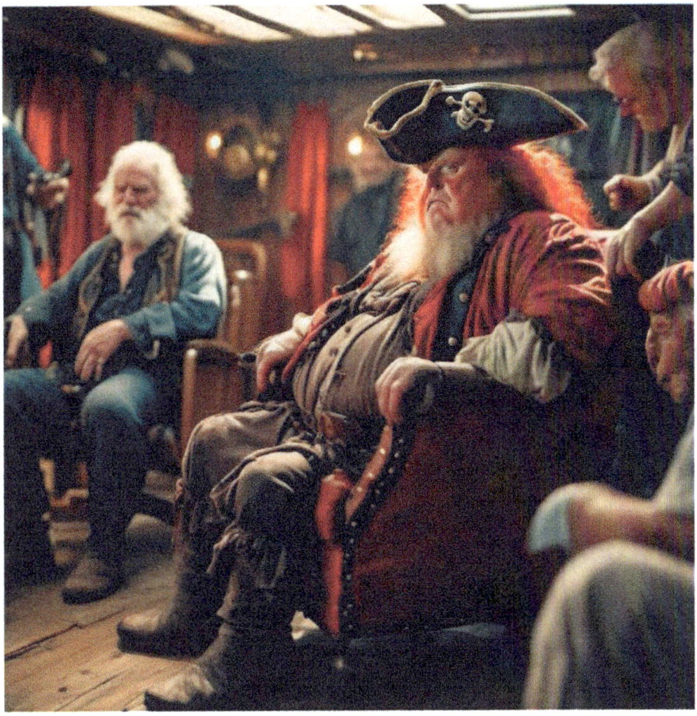

The jail cell dissolved, and I found myself confined in an even more sinister prison – a trailer home so narrow it felt like a coffin for the living. Twelve feet wide, the space was a testament to the geometry of despair, each cramped room flowing into the next in a suffocating progression: living room, kitchen bedroom, and back. The walls seemed to pulse with malevolent energy, closing in with each labored breath I took.

8 DAYS IN A COMA

This wasn't just any neighborhood. The airitself was heavy with the weight of broken dreams and desperate lives. The kind of place where hope comes to die, where drugs and crime write the rules of survival. Through the grimy windows, I could see other trailers, each one a mirror of my own prison, their occupants either oblivious to my presence or choosing to inore the hell unfolding in their midst.

8 DAYS IN A COMA

My captors – I couldn't bring myself to call them caretakers – were straight from the darkest corners of nightmare. The woman, with her red hair and thick glasses, looked like an angry puffer fish, her face perpetually contorted with disdain. Her eyes held no compassion, only a cold calculation that sent shivers down my spine. But it was the hillbilly who truly embodied the evil of this place. He was like something torn from the pages of a horror novel – long beard writhing like snakes around his face, eyes that seemed to glow with malicious Intent. His threat, delivered in a drawl that dripped with menace, still echoes in my nightmares: "I'm goanna make tobacco out of you." The words themselves were almost comical, but the intent behind them was pure evil. This wasn't just a threat of violence – it was a promise to reduce me to something less than human

Hmm… less than human. Where Am I?

JEREMY JUSTIN COOPER

They would dye my hair just like them and take me for walks, like a prisoner getting his yard time, parading me through the neighborhood in a wheelchair I couldn't escape. I'd scream at people in their yards, my voice raw with desperation: "Help me! This isn't right! I don't belong here!" But no one heard me. Or worse – they heard and didn't care. That's when the terrible truth hit me – this had to be hell, or at least a preview of it. A place where cries for help go unanswered, where evil masquerades as care, and where isolation becomes a physical weight pressing down on your soul.

JEREMY JUSTIN COOPER

The psychological torture was relentless.
"Your family doesn't want you anymore," they'd say, their voices dripping with false sympathy. "We took you from the hospital for your own good." Every word was designed to break my spirit, to sever my connection to Jennifer and my children, to make me accept this nightmare as my new reality. Behind the puke-colored
wallpaper, I discovered what seemed like a map – a possible escape route hidden
beneath layers of decay. The wallpaper itself was an assault on the senses, the
color of illness and despair.

JEREMY JUSTIN COOPER

Beneath it lay what looked like instructions, directions, a way out. But escape to where? In this reality, I wasn't just confined to a wheelchair; I was confined to a nightmare where even my most basic dignity was stripped away. The humiliation was constant. Soiling myself, being cleaned by people who took pleasure in my degradation, hearing their mockery – it was a different kind of restraint than the hospital ward or the jail cell. This was a prison of the spirit, designed to break not just the body, but the soul itself.

JEREMY JUSTIN COOPER

Yet even in this dark place, something inside me rebelled against their lies. I knew Jennifer wouldn't abandon me. I knew my kids wouldn't give up on me. Their love was my anchor to reality, even as this false reality tried to convince me otherwise. Each time my captors told me I was unloved, unwanted, I clung tighter to the truth I knew in my heart.

JEREMY JUSTIN COOPER

When my fist finally hit that wall, tearing through the map and the wallpaper, I wasn't just trying to escape the trailer – I was fighting for my very soul. The impact sent shockwaves through my entire being, and as the world began to dissolve around me once again, I realized each of these visions was teaching me something profound about faith, about love, about the choice between light and darkness. The trailer vanished, but the lesson remained: sometimes the narrowest places lead us to our broadest revelations about God's presence in our lives. In that confined space, surrounded by evil masquerading as care, I learned that faith could flourish even in the darkest corners of existence.

JEREMY JUSTIN COOPER

As consciousness slipped away once more, I understood that my journey through these realms was far from over. Each vision was a test, a lesson, a piece of a larger puzzle that would ultimately lead me back to life – but not before showing me truths about heaven, hell, and the precious space between them where souls hang in the balance.

JEREMY JUSTIN COOPER

Chapter 5:

Time's Twisted Mirror

JEREMY JUSTIN COOPER

The darkness lifted to reveal a Chicago hotel room in the 1990s, but something was terribly wrong with time itself. Models bustled through the corridors outside, their presence a bizarre backdrop to what should have been a simple family celebration. My old friend Artie was there, solid and real as the day I'd known him, but we were supposedly preparing for my cousin's wedding – a cousin who wasn't even born in the '90s.

JEREMY JUSTIN COOPER

The hotel Itself was familiar – I'd been there in my youth – but now it served as a stage for this impossible play of mixed timelines. My cousin Becca was getting married, but not in Chicago where we were, and certainly not in this decade. The real wedding would happen years later in Virginia or the Virgin Islands – yet here I was, trapped in this twisted version of events.

JEREMY JUSTIN COOPER

The hairdressers arrived, professional and efficient, their equipment spread out like surgeon's tools. They worked on my long hair – the same hair I had when my heart attack struck in 2022 – trimming and styling with practiced precision. But something was wrong. Very wrong.

JEREMY JUSTIN COOPER

"That's all the equipment we have. We're going home," they announced suddenly, packing up their tools.

"Wait!" I protested, panic rising in my throat. "You must be here for my cousin's hair. This is her wedding!"

Their response was coldly practical: "We took care of two people and were paid for two people. So, we're gone."

JEREMY JUSTIN COOPER

The weight of ruining my cousin's wedding crashed down on me – a wedding that existed only in this warped reality yet felt as real as my own marriage to Jennifer in 2016. The guilt was overwhelming, even though I knew somewhere in my mind that none of this made sense. I wasn't even invited to her real wedding, so how could I be here, in Chicago, in the wrong decade, ruining a ceremony that wouldn't happen for years?

JEREMY JUSTIN COOPER

The hotel room began to blur around" the edges, reality shifting like smoke in the wind. As consciousness slipped away once more, I realized these timeline jumps weren't random – they were teaching me something about regret, about family, about the choices we make and the ripples they create through time.

The last thing I saw before darkness claimed me was my reflection in the hotel mirror – but the face looking back wasn't from the '90s, or 2022, or any time I recognized. It was changing, aging, transforming into something else entirely. I was about to step into a future I never could have imagine.

JEREMY JUSTIN COOPER

CHAPTER 6:

SCREENS IN THE SKY

JEREMY JUSTIN COOPER

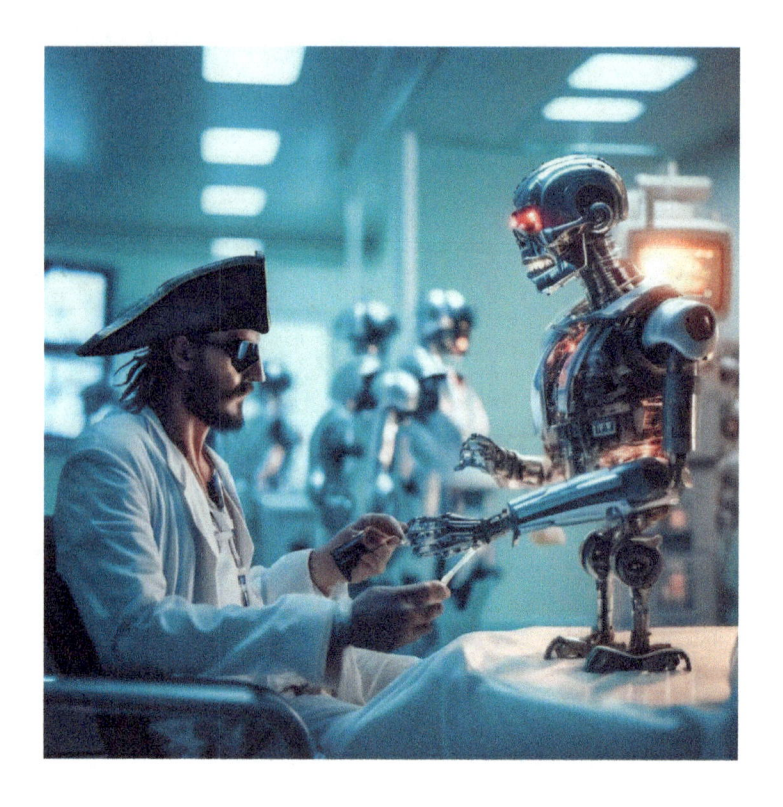

The future arrived like a slap to the face – stark, sterile, and impossibly advanced. The hospital room I found myself in wasn't just modern; it was something straight out of science fiction, perhaps a hundred years ahead of my time. The ceiling itself was alive with technology, smooth tiles transforming into interactive screens at the mere sound of my voice

JEREMY JUSTIN COOPER

Gone were the traditional TV channels – no ABC, no NBC, nothing familiar to ground me in reality. Instead, the entertainment system was something entirely different, more
immersive and somehow more unsettling. The ceiling became my window to this brave new world, responding to voice commands like some omniscient entity.

JEREMY JUSTIN COOPER

But what good was future technology when you couldn't even get a simple glass of milk? My throat burned with thirst, and in this high-tech prison, I discovered Ober still existed – or at least, some futuristic version of it. I tried repeatedly to order milk through Ober Eats, watching the delivery progress on the ceiling screen with desperate hope.

"Mr. Cooper," the nurse would appear on screen, her face stern and uncompromising, "you cannot have this." She'd disconnect me from the service, but like a man possessed, I'd find ways to reconnect, trying again and again to get that precious milk delivered. The robots that rolled through the corridors, performing tasks once done by human hands, seemed indifferent to my plight

8 DAYS IN A COMA

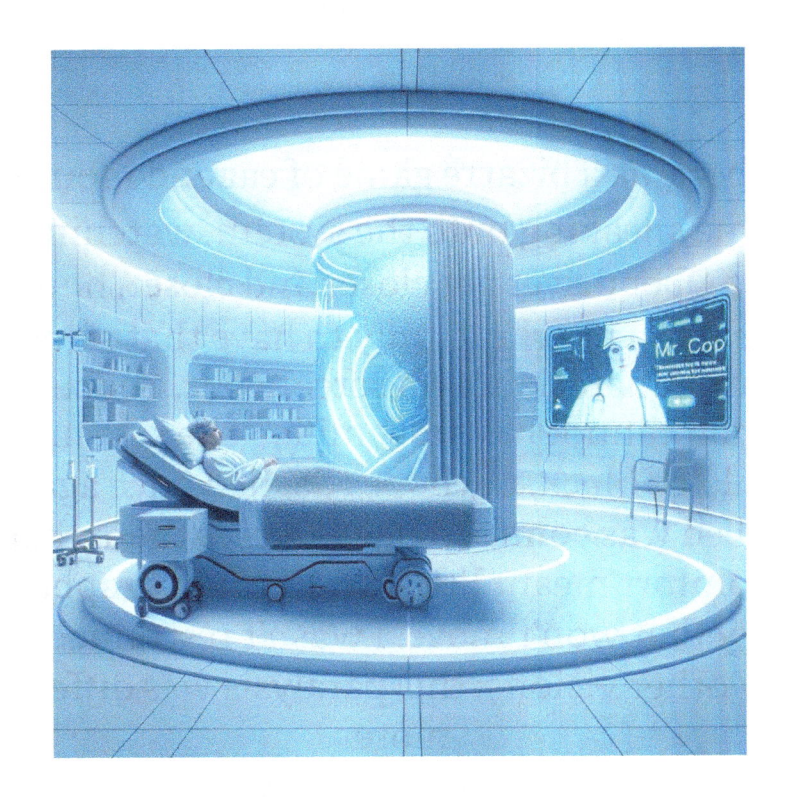

It became a bizarre game of cat and mouse – me sneaking onto the system, watching the Ober driver get closer and closer, hope rising in my chest, only to have that same nurse materialize on screen: "Mr. Cooper, you cannot have any milk." The screen would go black, my hopes dashed once again. The bed was comfortable – I'll give them that – but comfort meant little when you're trapped in a body that won't move. I wasn't restrained like in my other visions; this paralysis was different, more complete. Only my head would turn, allowing me to survey this sterile future where doctors were scarce, and computers made the decisions.

8 DAYS IN A COMA

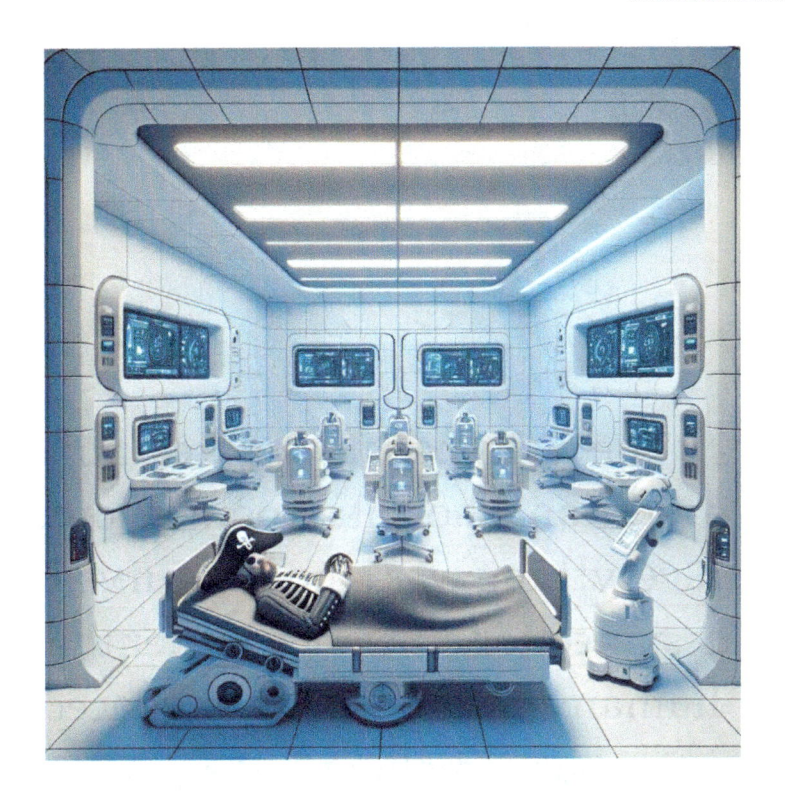

The walls had no squares, no traditional hospital room layout. Everything was smooth, curved, designed for efficiency rather than human comfort. It was advanced, yes, but somehow colder, more distant from the human touch that healing traditionally required.

8 DAYS IN A COMA

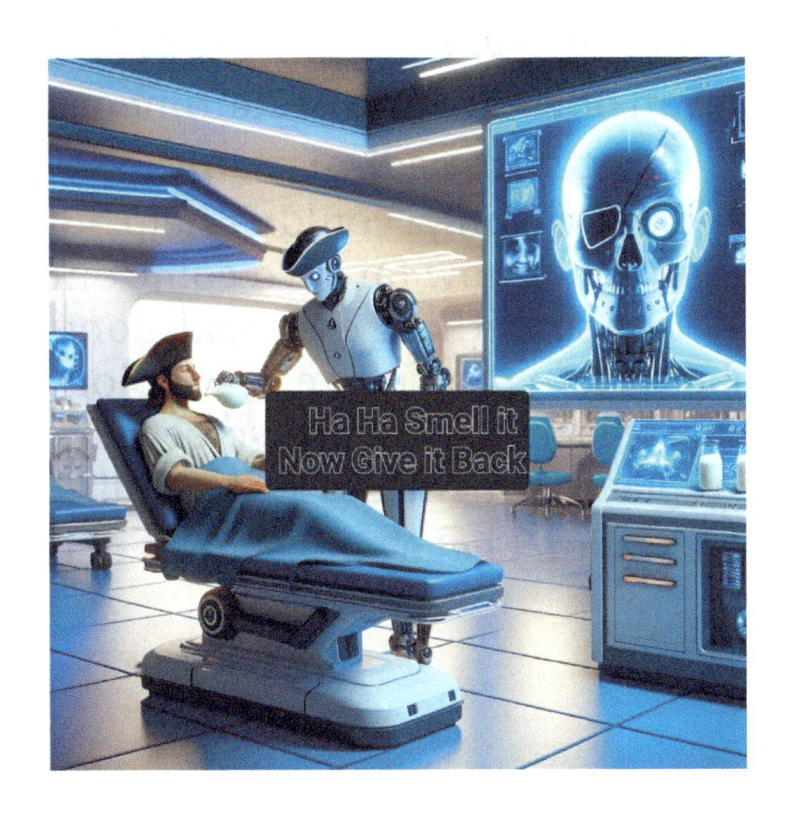

JEREMY JUSTIN COOPER

As I lay there, watching the ceiling
transform from entertainment
center to medical monitor
and back again, I couldn't help but
think about how far we'd come only
to lose something essential along
the way. In this future, technology
had replaced humanity, screens had
replaced touch, and still – still! –
a man couldn't get a simple glass of milk

8 DAYS IN A COMA

The future, It seemed, was just another
kind of prison – more comfortable
perhaps, but a prison, nonetheless. And as
the alarms
suddenly began to blare, red lights
pulsing across the ceiling screens,
I realized this vision had one more
lesson to teach me about the nature
of progress and the price we
pay for it…

8 DAYS IN A COMA

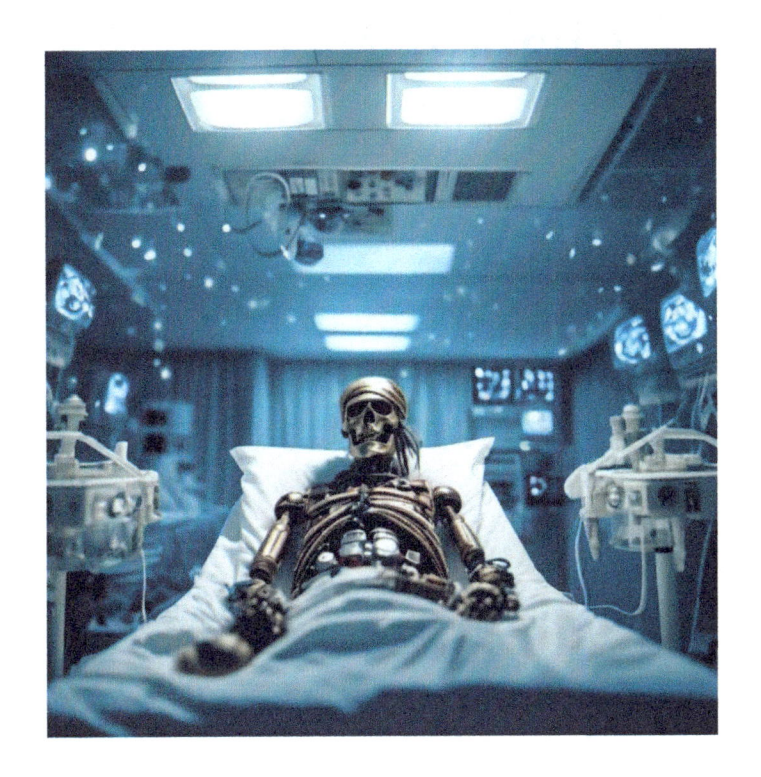

Chapter 7:

The
Devil's Power Outage

8 DAYS IN A COMA

The alarms in the futuristic hospital screamed their warning, red lights pulsing across the ceiling screens like digital blood. Through the chaos, I heard the panic in their voices: "They found us! They found us!" The fear was palpable, but something else was happening something miraculous.

8 DAYS IN A COMA

As the power failed and darkness swept through the facility, I felt sensation returning to my paralyzed body. First a tingling, then a surge of strength I hadn't felt since before my heart attack. The future's hold on me was weakening, its technological prison failing.

8 DAYS IN A COMA

In that moment of darkness, I heard it – the sound of pure evil, a voice that could only belong to the devil himself. "Stay down!" it commanded, trying to reconnect the emergency power, trying to trap me once again in this sterile hell. But I was done being a prisoner of time. "You are the devil!" I shouted, my voice finding strength I didn't know I had. "Get away from me!" Each word was a declaration of war against the darkness that had held me captive through so many timelines. My legs, frozen for what felt like eternities, finally responded to my will.

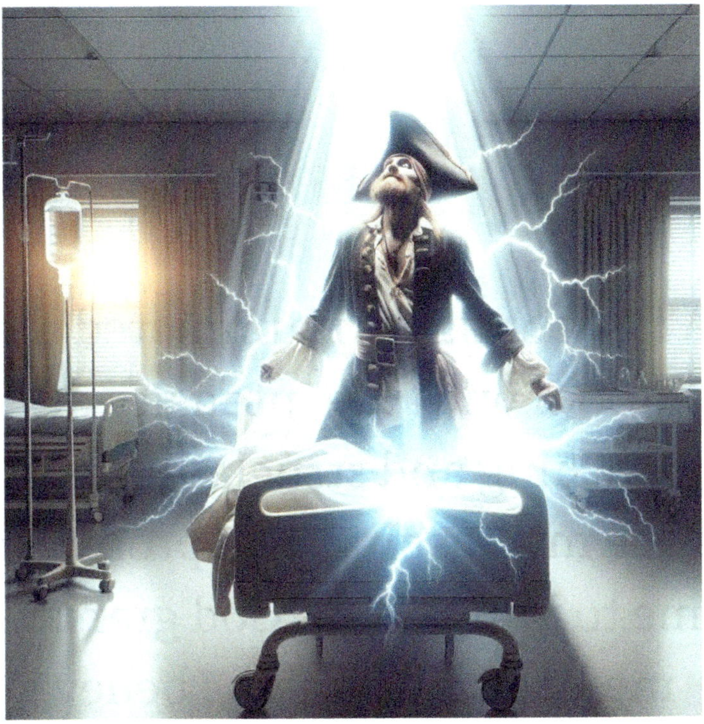

A flash of lights illuminated the room with the intensity of lightning and struck the devil beside my hospital bed, prompting me to jump out as God granted me strength, which I believe was his divine intervention.

8 DAYS IN A COMA

JEREMY JUSTIN COOPER

I ran. Through corridors that seemed to shift and change, past robots that stood lifeless without their power, past screens that no longer held my reflection. I ran until I burst through doors that opened onto a world I recognized – the steps of the Catholic Hospital, right next to Methodist where my physical body lay in 2022.

JEREMY JUSTIN COOPER

The February air hit my lungs like a blessing as I collapsed onto the snowy steps, my heart feeling like it might explode. "I want to go see the Lord," I gasped, the words torn from my soul. "I'm sorry for what I've done in the past. I'm sorry for not telling people about you. I'm sorry for believing and not believing and believing and all the time. Believing all the time."

JEREMY JUSTIN COOPER

My prayer continued, raw and honest: "Please stop this pain I'm going through right now. I want to see my wife and kids. I love them so much. Please let them have me if they will have me." That's when I heard her voice – the same nurse from my first vision, but now elderly, her face lined with decades of wisdom. "Do you remember me?" she asked, her smile gentle and knowing.

Recognition hit me like a thunderbolt. This was the same nurse I'd given investment advice to back in that 1930s hospital ward. But how…?

I'm the one you talked to back when I was in my late teens," she continued, "and told me what to do when the '60s '70s '80s and '90s stocks come around to make sure my family is okay." Her eyes sparkled with gratitude. "Because of that, my family will never ever have to endure any kind of hardship ever again. And neither will you."

8 DAYS IN A COMA

JEREMY JUSTIN COOPER

As I reached to hug her, overwhelmed by
the perfect circle God had drawn
through time itself, the world
began to shift one final
time. But this wasn't like the other
transitions – this was
different. This was…

JEREMY JUSTIN COOPER

I opened my eyes to see Jennifer's face, beautiful and tear-stained, looking down at me in my hospital room. Eight days had passed in the real world, though I'd lived lifetimes in between. My first words came without thinking:

"Are you dead too?"

JEREMY JUSTIN COOPER

TRUE LOVE

JEREMY JUSTIN COOPER

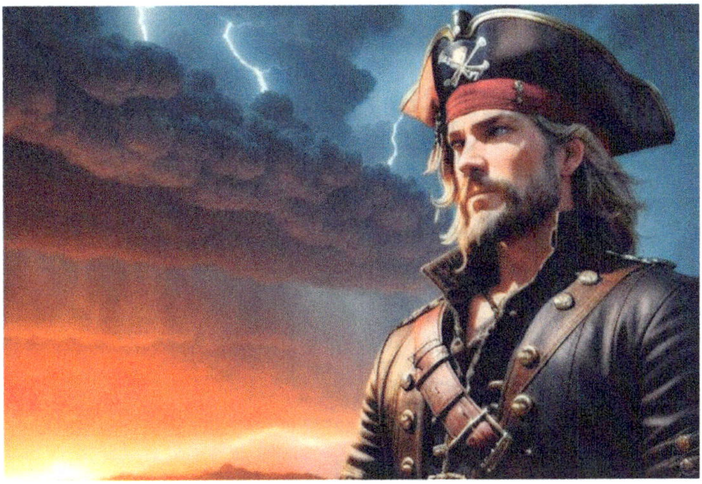

Chapter 8:

Treasures between Heaven or Hell

8 DAYS IN A COMA

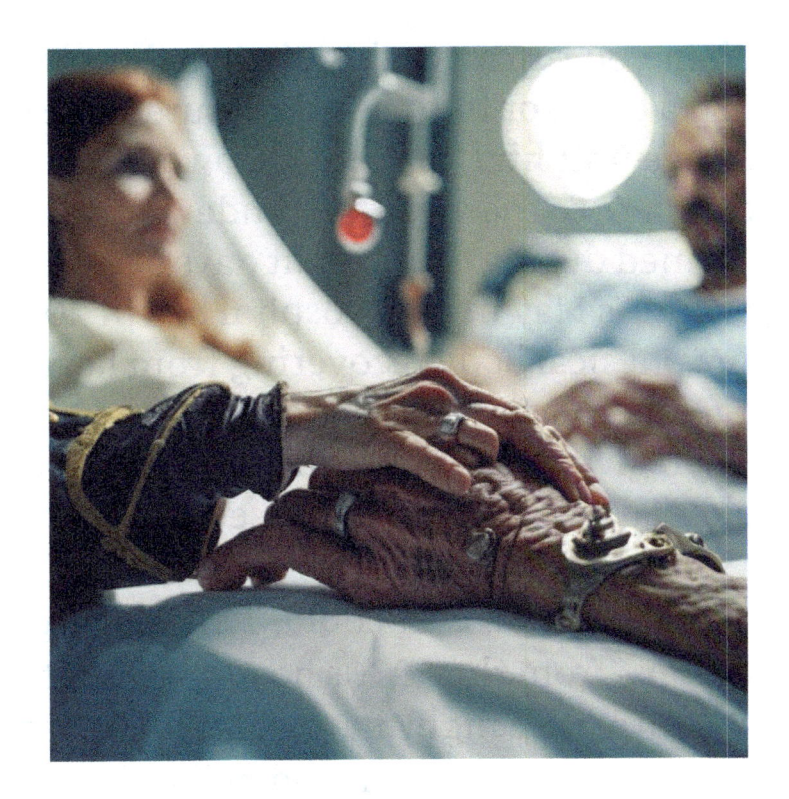

When you run an online pirate's shop, you learn a thing or two about treasures. But no storage unit find, no liquidation deal could compare to the wealth of understanding I gained during those eight days between worlds. As I lay in that hospital bed in 2022, my physical body recovering from heart surgery while Jennifer held my hand, I knew I'd been given something more valuable than gold – I'd been given a glimpse of the truth. Those eight days taught me what no Sunday sermon ever could. Through each vision – from the 1930s hospital ward to the futuristic nightmare – I learned that the linebetween heaven and hell isn't some distant boundary we cross when we die. It's a choice we make every day in how we live, how we love, and how we treat others.

8 DAYS IN A COMA

JEREMY JUSTIN COOPER

The kind nurse who appeared "both the beginning and end of my journey", showed me how our actions ripple through time. Just as my advice about Apple stock and Amazon investments helped secure her family's future.

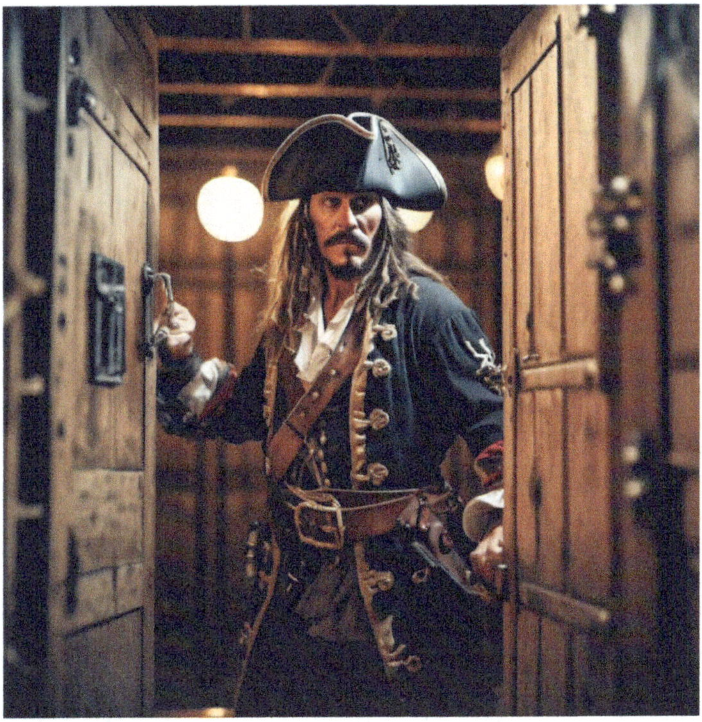

Every choice we make has consequencesthat stretch far beyond our understanding. power isn't about control – it's about using whatever influence we must help others. Like finding treasure in storage units, sometimes life's greatest discoveries come in unexpected places. My journey through different timelines wasn't just about being lost.

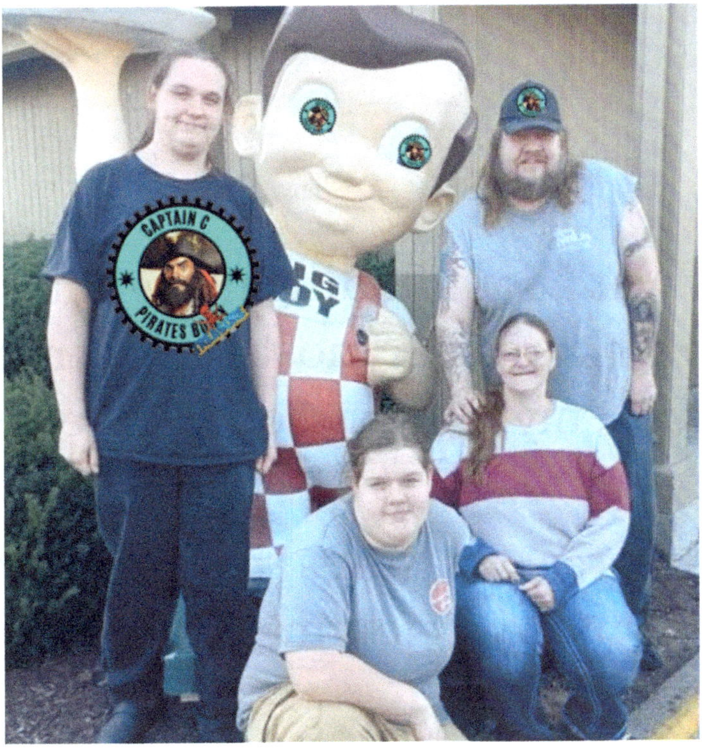
CAPTAIN C
PIRATES

It was about finding my way back to what matter most. Jennifer, my kids, my faith in God – these are

the real treasures that no thief can steal, no time can erode

8 DAYS IN A COMA

Running Captain C Pirates Booty has taught me about honest dealings and fair trades, but those eight days taught me something even more valuable – the importance of being honest with God. No more believing and not believing, no more walking the fence. Like a true entrepreneur, I had to make a decisive choice about
where I stood.

8 DAYS IN A COMA

The future I saw with its ceiling screens and robot caretakers showed me that all ourtechnological advances mean nothing if we lose our humanity in the process. Just as I strive to add that personal, pirate touch to every sale and every instructional video, we need to keep our faith personal and real. That elderly lady on the Catholic Hospital steps wasn't just a miracle – she was proof that God works in ways we can't comprehend, drawing perfect circles through time itself.

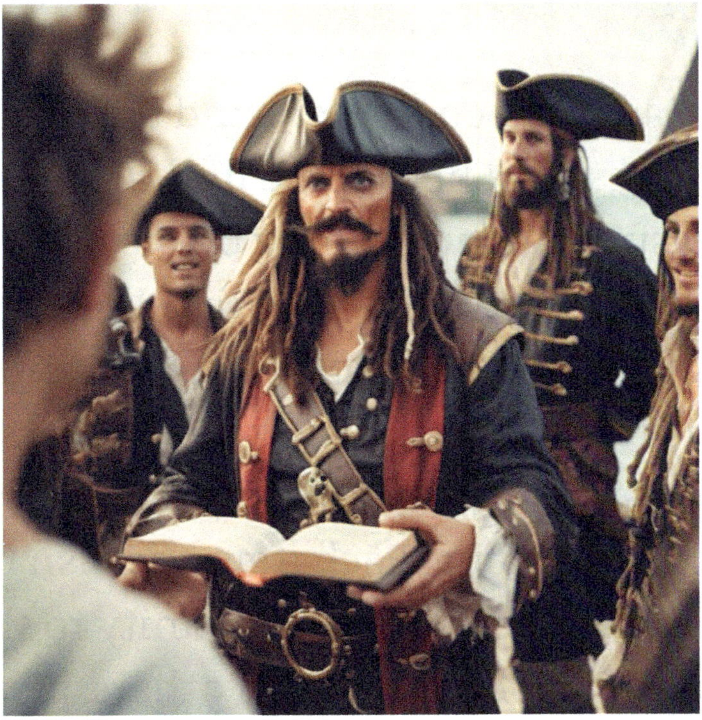

Just as I help customers find unexpected treasures, God helped me find the ultimate treasure understanding of His presence in every moment, every timeline, every choice. Today, as I continue building my business toward that dream of a brick-and-mortar thrift shop, I carry these lessons with me. Each item I sell isn't just merchandise it's an opportunity to share something of value with others, just as I'm sharing this story with you now

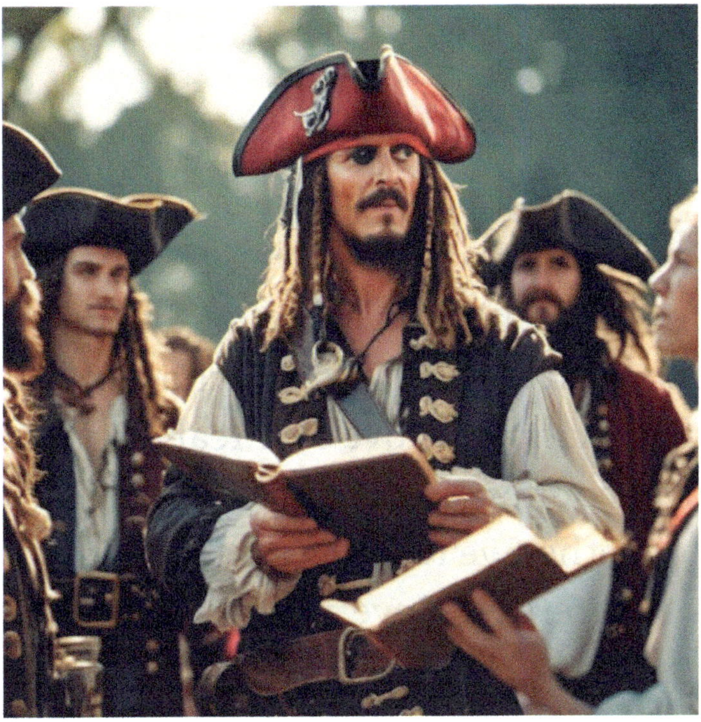

Those eight days between heaven and hell changed me forever. They taught me that faith isn't about perfection – it's about direction. It's about choosing light over darkness, love over fear, and truth over comfort. It's about recognizing that whether we're in the past, present, or future, God's love remains constant.

8 DAYS IN A COMA

JEREMY JUSTIN COOPER

To those reading this who might be walking that line between belief and doubt, I say this: don't wait until you're caught between worlds to make your choice. Heaven and hell are real, but so is God's love. Choose now. Choose faith. Choose life. Because sometimes the greatest treasure isn't what you find in a storage unit or sell in an online store. Sometimes it's what you discover when you're lost between worlds, fighting your way back to the light, guided by a love stronger than death itself.

JEREMY JUSTIN COOPER

And if you're wondering whether
this story is   true, just remember
every good pirate knows that the
most valuable treasures are   the
ones that transform your soul

Dedication

To my parents, who guided my ship through life's stormy waters,

Teaching me to navigate between right and wrong. Your steady hands at the helm helped chart the course that led me here. To my grandfather, who showed me the true compass of faith,

Pointing always toward the real God. Your wisdom continues to guide me through every voyage.

To my grandmother – my fellow soul of wonderful madness, Whose creative spirit matched my own wild adventures. Our shared "craziness" created a special bond that still makes me smile. I miss our adventures together, but your spirit sails on in my heart. To my sister, whose love and support has been a constant star In my journey through both calm seas and storms. And most precious of all – to Jennifer, my wife, my anchor, my North Star

Who married this pirate on April 16, 2016, And to William & Diamond the greatest treasures any father could ask for. Knowing that we'll sail together into Heaven when Jesus returns

Makes me the richest and happiest Captain on all God's seas. You are my greatest find, more valuable than any storage unit treasure. Together, you are the crew God blessed me with, and together we'll anchor in Heaven's harbor when He calls us home

WITH ETERNAL LOVE AND GRATITUDE,
Captain Jeremy Cooper

EPILOGUE:

A Pirate's Guide to Heaven and Hell

(And All Ports Between)

Ahoy, treasure seekers! You might be wondering what a pirate who sells storage unit finds and liquidation booty online learned from dancing between heaven and hell for eight days. Well, let me tell you – it's not the kind of

treasure map you'll find in your average storage unit! Some folks think being a "good pirate" is a contradiction in terms, but here I am – Captain Jeremy Cooper of Captain C Pirates Booty, living proof that God has a sense of humor.

After all, He took a guy who sells other people's forgotten treasures and showed him the greatest treasure of all – the truth about what lies beyond this world. Sure, I've found some amazing deals in storage units, but nothing compares to finding out that the nurse you gave stock tips to in the 1930s took your advice! Talk about a long-term investment strategy!

And while I might not be able to offer you Apple stock from the '80s, I can offer you something better – a reminder that God's timing is always perfect, even when it seems like you're trapped in a time traveling feverdream. These days, when I'm creating my pirate-themed product listings or making animated videos with my Captain's logo, I rememberthat futuristic hospital with its fancy ceiling TV. Let me tell you – all the technology in the world can't beat a simple glass of milk when you really need one!

To all my customers at Captain C Pirates Booty – yes, I'm still that same crazy pirate who makes shopping fun with animated videos. But now you know why I believe every treasure has a greater purpose, and why I treat each sale like it might just be part of God's bigger plan. Remember, mateys – whether you're browsing our online store or reading this book, you're not just looking for earthly treasures. You're part of a greater adventure. And this pirate captain can tell you firsthand – heaven is real, hell is real, and God's love is the greatest treasure of all.

Now, if you'll excuse me, I've got 14 items to post on Facebook and X, and these pirate-themed descriptions won't write themselves!

Sailing toward Heaven's harbor, Captain Jeremy Cooper

P.S. And no, I still haven't gotten that glass of milk from Ober Eats!

JEREMY JUSTIN COOPER

Made in the USA
Monee, IL
21 April 2025